THE KIND PRINCE

CHAPTER 1

A Purpose

MARISHA MUGUY

"Prince Christopher!" His guard Alfred as well as his right-hand-man calls out to him when he slips into his room after the encounter of the beautiful lady. "What in the blazing world were you doing?" Chris gives him a sheepish look with a tight nervous smile. "You snuck out again-" Alfred starts to yell but was cut off when Chris covers his mouth signaling for him to shut up.

"Shut it." He hissed.

Alfred removes Chris's hand from covering his mouth and shoots him a glare. "What the hell were you thinking? You could have been kidnapped and killed! Your parents' ball is starting soon too!" he whisper-yelled at Chris.

"I know. I know." Chris replies rolling his eyes at his guard's exaggeration. "You're overthinking it. I kept a low profile; they won't know it was me. See." He explains pulling up his hood, gesturing that no one can see his face.

Alfred groans, "They're going to find us dead one day and it's because of your foolishness." He mutters as his shoulders fall and lets out a frustrating sigh.

"Awe, come on Alfred, I'm not that bad." He pats Alfred's back.

"You have duties, stop fooling around and being a child. Your place isn't among the people; you're royalty and have responsibilities to attend to. Tonight your parents' are throwing you your coming of age party, and for once act your part as a prince." Alfred lectures as Chris takes a look at the cloths lain on his bed.

It was a black and green suit with matching trousers. Chris lets out a sigh as he takes a look. "I know Alfred, I get it. I'm a prince." He is a little irritated.

"I don't know why you are doing it like that. You're a prince, you have everything and the life everyone wants." Alfred questions. You always act like there's something more you want. What more could you possibly want, you have it all compared to others. Alfred thought to himself.

With a longing look Chris gazes out of the doors of his balcony. "Sometimes you have it all when truly you have nothing at all." He says, "Like a desert mirage, my fortune is nothing. It's just a figment of my imagination." He says as he heads to his bathroom to bathe. Then he pauses as he opens the door to his bath and tilts his head to face Alfred. "Sometimes a smile is a silent cry, my friend."

Alfred stood speechless; it was rare for Chris to act mature for real. It's one of those times he drops his mask and every time he does Alfred is always left speechless.

You poor soul, who would have known such a joyful child goes through so much. I've stood by him for as long as I can remember. When I was 10 father took me here and told me to protect the third prince and the third prince's treasure when he was 5 years old. At first as a child I thought he meant the prince and his fortune. But when his older sister died of an incurable disease 6 years later something happened to him.

His father, mother, and brothers cried by his sister's coffin when he stood to walk in front of his family. Tears were falling from his eye down his cheeks and his falls from his chin as he faces them. "Big sister, please don't worry. I'll keep you awake; you won't sleep as you do. I'll always remember my sister what you told me." He kisses her cheek and turns to his family. He wipes his tears but more just pours as he watches his family whip. "Let's go to the rose garden!" He says as he smiles through his pouring tears.

Everyone looked at him surprised and shocked. "Your sister is dead and you want to go play?" His father glares fiercely.

But Chris doesn't flinch and more tears begin to pour a lot more. His lips tremble but he fights for a smile and bites down a sob. "She's not dead yet father, she's asleep, but finally she's free."

"What do you mean!? Your sister is dead, can't you see!?"His mother screams through sobs as everyone starts rumbling.

"Be quiet!" he silenced the crowd and only the mourns of his family and close people were heard. Before smiling at his family, "Would big sister want you to cry?" He asked softly. The question stung everyone into silence. "If big sister were here she'd say, 'this is the worst funeral ever! Everyone is wearing black, why couldn't they wear blue or green. Why is everyone crying, I don't want my last memory with you guys so sad! Come on, smile.' Yeah, something like that." Everyone was still quiet so he continued. "Before my big sister died she made me promise to smile at her funeral and to make sure everyone smiled." Everyone was now relaxed listening to the little boy. "Or else she's risen up and stole my toys."He says as he pouts and every one chuckles. "Carlo I don't know what it means but she told me to tell you, 'If you wait the beautiful little birdie will leave before you even give her some hearts.' Chasten, big sister said to give you this." He says as he hands his brother an envelope. "Mother and Father, big sister said that she's sorry, she didn't mean to go away. But she'll always be with you as long as you remember her."

His mother then turns and sobs into her husband's chest. "Oh Karin, my sweet, sweet princess momma forgives you!"

That day was a devastating day for everyone, but it was more painful for him. Princess Karin was practically a mother to him as well as a sister. She raised him herself. I mean come on, giving a kid like him such an important role. The pressure's just too much...but still, how is he smiling? The thought himself as right on cue Chris comes out in his suit and trousers with a bright smile that you can't help but find yourself returning. "Let's go Alfred! Father is surely going to kill me now." He says with a chuckle.

"Yeah, let us depart." Alfred opens the door for his master.

The Third Prince of Castidon made his way to the ball with his guard not knowing what's to come. On the other end Lady in wait Miss Selene Trison accompanies her majesty Princess Lacy of Torronian to the ball.

****

"Lacy!" An acquaintance of the princess calls out from behind them as she and Selene make their way to the ball.

The princess looks behind them, "Miriam! It's been forever!" She gushes as she walks over to Princess Miriam as they hug and kiss each other's cheeks. "Are you here for the third prince's coming of age ball too?" Lacy asks.

"Uh huh! I heard he was quite the looker as well as charming!" They gushed over the topic.

Selene doesn't make any interruption nor pays much attention to what they are saying as they kept walking.

"Yes, I've also heard that he could pick a bride today." The gossip and squeak in excitement as they entered the ballroom filled with princes' and princesses' and other important ladies and gentlemen. Selene's mind was still occupied by the earlier event that happened with the stranger on the way to the palace. With her mind clouded she excused herself to the dinner table with a glass of wine in hand.

With her clouded mind she clumsily bumps into a group of young men. "I'm sorry." She mutters with her head down as she tries to walk around them. With no luck the one she bumped into pulls her towards him slipping his hand around her waist.

"You think you can bump into me and get away with just a sorry?" The guy brings her to close for her liking as she struggles to try and get away. "She's a pretty little thing. We should punish her." He says to his friends.
"I said I was sorry. I wouldn't do it again, I promise." She whimpers as she looks around to see no one was paying attention.

"Yeah she's a pretty one." They ignored her as one of them picked up a strand of her golden locks to sniff it.
Before they could continue they were interrupted. "Are we interrupting anything boys?" A voice speaks from behind them.

Earlier
"Hey Alfred" Prince Christopher taps Alfred to gain his attention as he points to Jacob and his group of thugs. "It looks like the rat is causing trouble again." He glares at the group.
Alfred glares too as they made their way to the group to see them man-handling a lady. "Am I interrupting anything boys, Sir Pete?" Alfred says, directing his glared at the leader who held the lady.

Pete rolls his eye and sends a glare back. "Yes you are, now leave you filthy dog. Go back to sucking up to that pathetic excuse of a prince of yours." As soon as he says the last sentence he feels an intense glare at the back of his head which sent shivers down his spin making him sweat.

Selene feels the hand around her waist tense as she looks up at Pete's posture to see him tense up.

Pete was then shoved from behind startling him as he stumbles and loses hold of Selene. Selene then runs behind Alfred in fear.

Pete was spun around to be face to face with Chris who pulled him by his collars. With a fierce and terrifying glared he growls under his breath. "On you mean this pathetic excuse of a prince you say? You have a lot to say. Why don't you pay for your sins against me?" He growls at him in a taunting whisper.

Pete was now very scared. "You shouldn't have called him pathetic, and adding prince was just icing for yourself." Alfred mutters.

"Oh Prince Chris, Your Majesty, sorry I-I d-didn't see y-you there." Pete stutters, but only receives a fiercer glare. "I'm so sorry your majesty, it won't happen again." He lowers his head in submission.

"Am I the only one you should be sorry to? I did see you harass a beautiful young lady and insulted my right-hand-man at my party, in my palace; tell me...what should become of you?" He hissed.

Pete and his mates turned towards Alfred and Selene giving a slight bow then back to me. "We're really sorry." They say.

"You better be, because next time I won't be so kind." He says then gesture them away. Then he turned to get a better look at the lady. It's the girl from before, he thought to himself. He was about to greet her 'Hello again' but then thought about keeping this a mystery. "It's alright right now." He sticks out his hand for hers.

A bit hesitant at first, she finally places her hand in his. Alfred sees the actions unfold in front of him and decides to give them privacy. "Well your majesty I shall excuse myself." He bid goodbye to both of them.

He was gorgeous, this prince who had saved her from those men. His jet black hair looked as though he just came out of the shower and didn't put much effort into fixing it, but still somehow managed to pull the look off. Though what captivated her was the young prince's jaded green eyes. She found them quite familiar as she gazed into them, but from where she couldn't place a finger on.

"Are you alright?" A voice brings her back to reality, for she had not known she had been staring at the prince for long now. She only managed to nod at his question which caused him to chuckle. "You're so beautiful." He says with another chuckle as he tucks a loose strand behind her ear before giving her a genuine smile.

The action itself caused her cheeks to turn crimson red and her heart skip a beat. "Thank you, you look handsome too." She mutters shyly causing the prince to let out a soft laugh.

"What's your name princess?" He asks as he leads her to the dance floor with no refusal.

She shakes her head with a frown and sighed. "My name is Selene Trison and I am no princess your majesty." She lowers her gaze to the ground. He laces their fingers together and starts to dance.

"Hm...Is that so? Would you want to be a princess, Selene?" He asks softly as they start to sway with the music.

The way he said her name was music to her ears as she nodded. "Not that it'd be any use, but yes I would like to be a princess."

Chris smiles at her honestly. "Then you shall be my princess tonight, Princess Selene."

As soon as the song ended Chris feels a tap on his shoulder. He turned to see his mother the Queen. "Yes mother?" He questions still not unlacing his fingers from Selene's.

"This is Princess Lacey from the Torronian Kingdom overseas." She gestured to the brunette beside her.

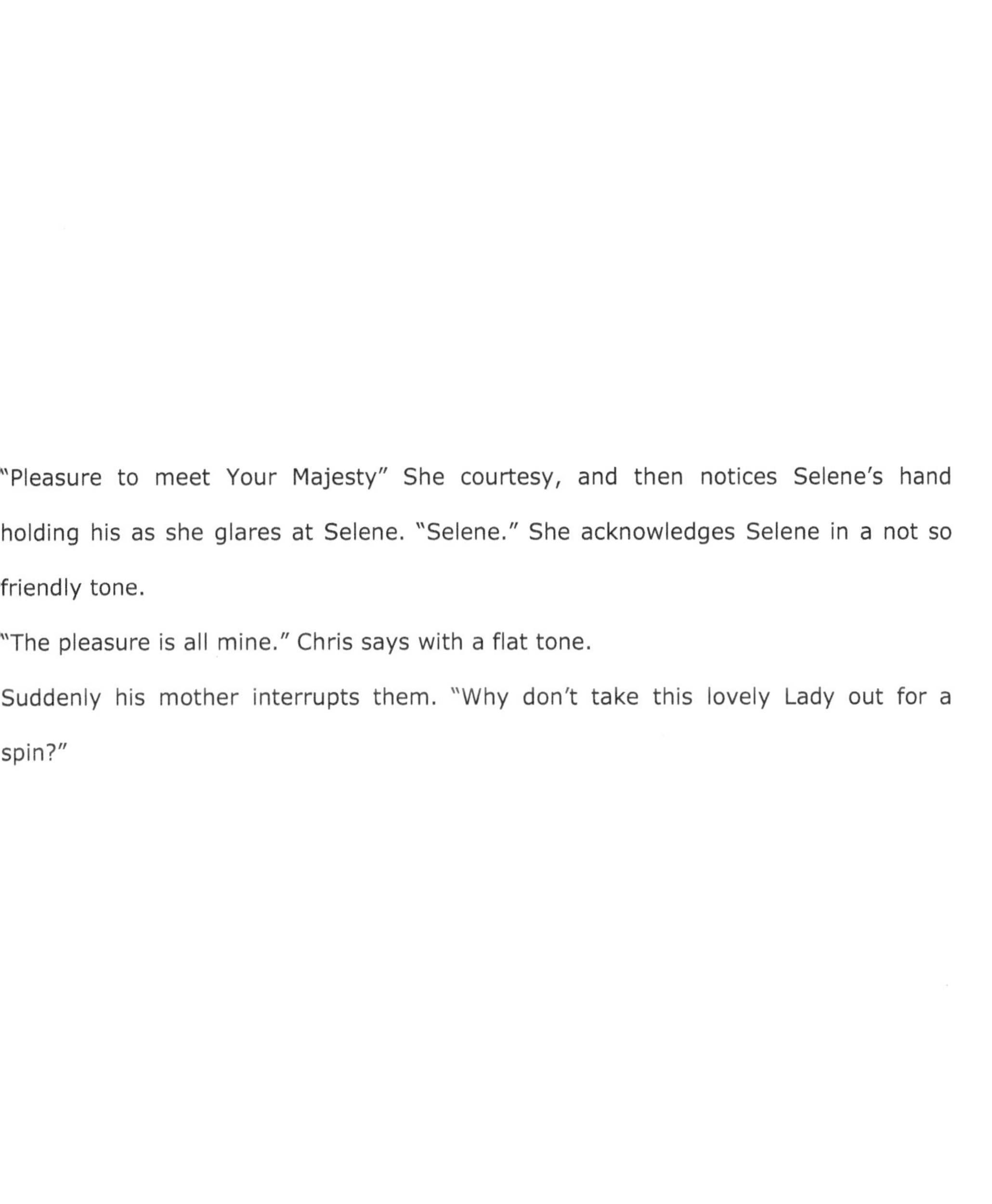

"Pleasure to meet Your Majesty" She courtesy, and then notices Selene's hand holding his as she glares at Selene. "Selene." She acknowledges Selene in a not so friendly tone.

"The pleasure is all mine." Chris says with a flat tone.

Suddenly his mother interrupts them. "Why don't take this lovely Lady out for a spin?"

Selene felt Lacy's smug look and she didn't ever raise her head. She didn't know why but she didn't like the fact that Chris was with the type of girl Lacy was. She felt Chris's hand grip hers in reassurance as she raised her gaze to meet him.

"I'll be back." He places a kiss on her knuckles causing heat to rise to her cheeks. The action itself made Lacy wish Selene six feet underground. "Promise to not get into anymore trouble okay." Chris softly says and much too both their disappointment released her hand.
"It's not like I get into it ever so often." Selene rolled her eyes.

The sentence itself brought a sly smile onto his face when he recalled that she does not know that event that took place from before. "Oh you do, my princess." He says in a whisper only she can hear as he leaves her and goes to Lacy's side.
As he left her standing there with her heart thumping she couldn't help but think back to when that mysterious man made her feel when he swooped down and saved her from harm.

Leaving her stunned as always brought a smug grin to his face as he walked away.
The amusement and interest were gone from Chris's eyes when he led Lacy to dance.
Lacy had not liked the fact that Chris wasn't acting the way he was acting with Selene when he danced with her. She had overheard their conversation so she decided to confront him while they danced. "Selene is not a princess." She stated.

"I know." He flatly replied.

"Then why did you call her a princess?" She demanded.

Chris was starting to get annoyed with Lacy. "I am not obligated to you Princess Lacy, it is none of your concern how I decide to live my life." He gives her a sharp look.

Lacy flinches, as she becomes angry. "But Prince Chris, why do you look at her with that look but not me." She demanded again.

"In my eyes Selene is an image of grace and elegance, and everything a princess should possess, but you Princess Lacy are no princess, no matter your birthright. Being bratty and spoil is no character a princess should possess." With that said the music ends and Prince Chris walks away from her. Pausing for a moment he turns to look her dead in the eye. "She's more of a princess then you'll ever be." And then disappears into the crowd.

Lacy stood there in her spot frozen and furious.

When Chris had come to look for Selene he found her already dancing with another fellow, who smiled and laughed with her as they danced. Chris didn't like the fact that someone else was making her happy, but he did like the fact that she was enjoying the party a bit more.

What he said to Lacy earlier about Selene was true. She was a picture of perfection, tonight she had wore a baby blue dress that complemented her beautiful eyes. The dress complemented her eyes, and her hair was pinned in a messy bun at the back of her head with fancy pins.

She moved gracefully across the dance floor as she swayed, her loose strands bounced off of her shoulders and on again, and her smile never once faltered. She was perfect, and the prince soon found himself unable to take his eyes of the radiant beauty.

Across the room as she danced she caught Chris watching her as he gave her a slight smile. She was about to excuse herself from her acquaintance but then looked back and found him gone from his spot. Where could have Chris gone? She thought to herself. Shrugging she continued on dancing.

"It has seemed the third crowned Prince of Castidon fancies of you." Her dancing partner says with an eyebrow raise.

She gave him a confused shocking look. "W-what?" She stutters out. "What possessed you to think that?"

"Don't give me that look; he has been eying you throughout the whole dance." He says with an eye roll. It's pretty obvious to everyone here. He thought to himself as he looked about.

"It's nothing like that, Chris and I aren't—" She starts but was interrupted.

"He lets you call him by that?" He asked for shock.

"Yes, it's no big deal. Doesn't he let anyone call him that?" She asked.

"Other than people he cares deeply about he doesn't let anyone at all. Princess Miriam is a close friend of the kingdom but he never let her call him that."

This brought heat to her cheeks. "Strange" She mumbles with a shy smile. Really strange. She thought to herself as she thought of the possibilities to come.

The dance had soon come to an end and Selene still hadn't seen the Prince through the rest of the evening. She sighed. Maybe he left early? She thought to herself as she made her way to the princess she had previously come in the company of.

As she approached Lucy, the princess furiously shot her glare. "Oh so the ungrateful lamb decided to come back to the master?" Lucy snares.

Selene sighed tiredly, "Princess, what has this ungrateful maid done that is not to your liking?" Selene spoke with such sarcasm low under her voice.

"You stole my spotlight! You useless thing! Let's be on our way! I'll punish you when we get home!" Lucy threw a fit as she dragged Selene by the arm.

A carriage has already been well prepared for the nobles and their invites for safe travel home.

But no one knew what was waiting for them on the way home. As they reached their destination Lucy immediately ran into the palace frantically yelling. "Mother! Father!" Lucy called out to them as she ascended the stairs.

Selene shortly followed behind till she stopped behind Lucy who came to a sudden halt. Selene with her head held low confusingly waited for Lucy to do something. In confusion she looked ahead of her to Lucy. To her surprise Lucy was trembling furiously.

"Lucy? Um, what's the matter?" Selene reached out with her hand. Although something stopped her, something insightful and horrifying. The smell of rot was strong carried in the breeze and in front of the doors of the throne room were dead servants and guards. The scene played in their heads over and over till they finally realised the reality. Lucy broke out in a scream, falling to her knees with tears in her eyes.

Selene trying to hold it together stepped forward, walking towards the door dodging dead bodies on her way. Taking a deep breath she pushed the door open, but what she saw was as bad as what was outside. Body parts were everywhere, flesh and blood as fresh on the ceiling and there on the throne was the king and queen. A looming shadow was casted over them.

"Your Majesties?" Selene called out before Lucy ran past her and jumped into her parents arms, only for them to go limp and cold.

"Mother? Father?" Lucy shook them in rage and confusion, hoping and wishing deeply it isn't what it is. She shook them hoping it was all a prank till her mother fell from the throne. On her back was a big clean cut coated in blood.

Selene silently mourned for her king and queen as she took a look around to see a familiar body. Taking a step forward she discovered it was her mother's. As she stared at her mother's soulless eyes she sighed, "All your hard work comes to this?" She asked the dead. She didn't feel any sadness or happiness for what has become of her mother, just pity.

Before anything else could be done, footsteps were heard. "We've finished with the royal family yet the princess is still not found." The voice muttered as they neared the throne room.

Selene rushed to Lucy hastily and grabbed her by the hand. "Lucy their coming for you, come." Selene whispered in a rush as she dragged her to the balcony.

"What now?" Lucy sobbed out the words a bit louder than they both wanted.

The footstep came to a halt as they heard one of the men. "Did you hear that Claude?"

"Yes." A deep voice reply. "It's coming from the balcony."

The footstep came closer and closer to the door, what were they supposed to do? They were on the third story of the palace. Selene frantically looked around searching for an escape for them. Her eyes landed on the pool of water below. It's a gabble we have to take. She thought to herself as she grabbed Lucy's hand and both got up on the edge ready to jump.

"Lucy you have to trust me." Selene spoke strongly. Lucy only nodded in response before the doors of the balcony flew open.

"Grab them!" One of the men yelled out, but they were too late, both ladies had already taken a leap of faith.

Back at the palace where the clueless prince lay awake thought back to how he told her to leave without a goodbye. "Ugh!" He groans before getting up and dressing up. "Just another runaway, I'll be back...in maybe a few days after crossing the country." Chris mumbles to himself before securing his sword to his hip.

Should I take the balcony? Or kill the palace wall? Ah, I'll walk through the front door. The prince thought to himself as he reached for the door, and opened it to find Alfred.

"Chris..." He spoke sharply with a glare. "Where do you think you're going in the middle of the night." Alfred questioned as he took in runaway attire.

Chris was caught red handed and he nervously tried to find a way around him. He sighed, "Looks like I'm taking the balcony." He spoke as he started to close the door.

"Oh no you're not!!!" Alfred yelled out loud calling the guards as he tried to hold the door open.

Chris manages to shut the door behind him as he runs for the balcony, leaping off the edge to a nearby tree. He skillfully made his way down as he dashed for the castle gates. By the gate 2 guards were patrolling on horse when Chris jumped in front of them startling the horse. The guards fell off the horse with so little time to react to the fact that the prince stole one of their horses.

As he rode for his freedom, not far behind him were Alfred and his guards. "Catch the prince!!" Alfred roared in frustration. "Chris!!"

Determined to escape he rode for the city's gates. Realizing what Chris was about to do he held out to the guard, "Close the gates! Close the gates!!!"

"HIYAH!" Chris charges his horse full speed for the gates. And before anyone knew it Chris pushed past the gates before they were fully closed. Finally past the gates he stopped to catch his breath. Alfred and the guards were on the other side glaring at him, but the prince was so proud of his successful escape. He turned to Alfred and said, "I'll be back in a few days!!" He shouted before he rode towards the direction Selene's carriage went.

After 4 hours of riding he finally arrived at the gates of Galisia. To his surprise the city was a wreck, the gates were torn down, knights and soldiers were dead as were innocent civilians. Looking ahead of him he saw the palace burn, in a state of panic he thought of Selene.

Where could she have gone, is she still alive? Terrified of what he may find he made his way to the castle. What he discovered was a massacre of the whole royal family, but not a slight sign of the princess and Selene.

A bit of hope sparked when he found the ribbon that was once on Selene. Still he was left in the dark, till he saw something else. Along with were the howls and barks from hounds and shouts from people. He looked below to the pool to see a wet trail.

He chuckles in relief knowing that they actually jumped and he has just a bit of time. A bit of time for what? Too save a princess and the girl he seems to have such fancy in. Finally a more exciting and adventurous purpose. As he rode following the howls and men yelling, he finally could spot them. Looking past the rushing men he saw 2 lady figures.

His heart beat started to pick up. Please be her, please be her. He begged for his thoughts. As his hopes built up he rode past the hooligans, shoving them out of his path. Finally catching up with the 2 he stopped a couple feet in front of them.

To his disappointment it wasn't them, but nonetheless he decided to help the 2 ladies. "Hurry up!" He got off to help the other two, only for them to run away with the horse as soon as they settled on. "Goddamn it!" He shouts as he brings out his sword. Stay fucking calm, it's the only way out. Ugh those ungrateful bitches! He thought to himself as he composes himself, till he saw the number he was up against. "Yeah, nah...I'm not fighting an army." With those few words he was running for his life with the men hot on his heels.

After a few minutes of running he finally lost them. Leaning on a tree to catch his breath he sighs in frustration. "Ugh", he groans when he hears footsteps. "What? They found me already?" He breathlessly complains till he looks up in front of him.

"Prince?" The person questioned was confused.

Selene and Lucy have been on the run and have lost the villains. "Ah, finally we lost them." Selene sighed and looked at Lucy. Lucy was still shell shocked from seeing her parents dead.

Tears fell from Lucy's eyes, she cried and sobs till she felt an arm come around her. "Selene...this isn't a dream is it?" Lucy questioned in tears hoping everything would just end.

Selene shook her head despite knowing that Lucy couldn't see her. To the response Lucy knew this was all real. Her parents really are dead, she has no home, and she's all alone. Selene sympathized with her and held her still she calmed down, but in the midst of their mourning they heard pounding footsteps.

"Shhhh." Selene covered Lucy's mouth with her hand. She picked up the nearest rock and signaled Lucy to be quiet and wait. Stepping out of the bushes to attack the person she found herself looking at someone she didn't expect in a place such as that. There slouching by a tree was the prince. "Prince?" She questioned.

Their eyes met and both were filled with so much relief. "Selene?" Chris spoke with so much hope. Selene nodded in reassurance.

"What are you doing here your highness?" She curtsy after realizing he was indeed the prince and a royal.

"Selene who is it?" Lucy spoke weakly as she stepped out. Seeing who it was she gasps. "Oh your highness! You came for me didn't you?" She sobbed and threw herself into the arms of the prince as Selene stood by helplessly.

The prince sympathized with the princess, "I'm sorry for your lost princess. We have a place for you and Selene at the palace if you have nowhere else to go."

Although the prince knew nothing of what he was inviting into his home, Selene did. Due to Lucy's personality and the fact that she is very delicate, a simple kindness will make her feel deeply dependent towards you.

Before they could decide on what to do next an arrow was shot towards the prince and Lucy. Still caught in the moment they didn't see it coming, but Selene did. Instinctively she rushed to push them out of the arrows' way, although she succeeded she wasn't able to get away fast enough because the arrow had pierced her in her back shoulder.

Blood gushed out of Selene's shoulder as she urged the two, "Go, I'll hold them off. You both would be able to make it further without an injured person." She spoke as she coughed up blood.

In a desperate state Lucy grabbed the prince's hand and fled with him, much to Selene's discomfort. Getting up on her feet she hid the rock behind her back. Wishing for not the safety of the Princess, but the Prince she called out. "Stop hiding in the shadows!" She growled in pain and frustration.

The person spoke in the shadows, "You are weak. Oh look the Princess you had saved had repaid you by abandoning you." The person steps into view with a smirk on her face. "I can help you get what you want." She spoke as she stepped closer.

She trembled as the lady got closer. "How could you possibly know what I want?" She asked the mysterious person.

"Oh but my dear, I do." She laughed. "I saw it in your eyes when she flung herself into his arms." She chuckles maliciously. "Awe, poor, poor Selene, you devoted your entire life to the princess and she runs away with the man you want." She says in mock pity, before bursting into a fit of malicious giggles.

"You're wrong!" Selene hissed. "Chris is only my friend, I just met him!" She reasons, but the lady shook her head in sympathy.

"I know the look of adoration when I see it. I've been there too sweetheart." She spoke with such fake frowns. "Men don't respect us dear. Not unless we have power, and I can give you that." She spoke seriously with a devilious air around her.

"No don't listen to her!!!" Chris interrupted before Selene could even answer.

Chris had long left Lucy at a lake not so far from them and had then ran after his damsel. Both Selene and the unknown lady were both stunned by the unexpected arrival.

Finally realizing Chris wa shere and Lucy wasn't, Selene panicked. "Where's the princess!?" Selene lashes out.

The prince was surprised by the way he reacted to him being here, and actually trying to save her life. "Don't worry she's safe." He says in defeat before moving to shield her from the Lady. "What do you want?"

"I just want to eradicate everyone, the whole royal family and everyone related to them." She said with a smile that said she wasn't kidding.

"Then why are you here, why are you targeting Selene?" Chris asked with his guard up.

The lady tapped her chin and thought for a moment before she spoke. "Um I don't know. Maybe because she's the king's illegitimate daughter. Born to one of the kings hookups, Lady Micheal."

"What?" Selene asked, unable to process what was said. "You're lying." She spoke accusingly.

The Lady tilted her head with a smile, "What? You didn't know?" she spoke with a cynic. "Awe, poor, poor Selene, you thought your 'father' treated you like crap because he didn't like your performance? No, he didn't like the fact that you weren't his daughter. Did you ever wonder why such a low rank baron could have so much wealth? It's because the king paid them to stay quiet." She spoke in a matter of fact way before she giggled in false innocence.

Selene by then with all this information and the bleeding she collapsed on her knees. "This can't be...no." She held her head as she quivers.

Chris glared at the lady with not an ounce of trust. "Where do you get your source?" He demanded as he pointed his swords at her.

The lady chuckles, "Are you doubting me?" she asked in disbelief. "Because if you do...I don't really care." She spoke with not a trace of playfulness she once had. "Now give me the girl, prince." She spoke pulling out a dagger pointing it at him.

"Never." He spoke as he shields the still shocked Selene.

The lady then snapped her fingers and in a second 2 huge men stepped out of the bushes. "Boys...get them." she ordered as they unsheath their swords.

The first guy leaped into the air and swung his sword down trying to slice Chris in half. Luckily he dodge just in time, but there's no time to rest. The other guy soon came at him thrusting his sword forward going for his side. The prince was able to block it with his own sword before acting back. He gave the first guy a roundhouse kick in the skull before ducking when the other swung his sword wildly.

The first guy had stumbled back into a neat by tree holding his head. Blood dripped from his skull as he spit out a whole bunch of them and saw a few of his teeth that were knocked out. "You little bastard! I'll get you for this." He yelled as he gripped his sword. He threw himself at Chris in rage as he thrust his sword forward.

Matching the first guy's act, the second guy aimed for his backside. Dodging the first blow and barely avoiding the other one he stumbled back a little. He groans when he's hell gets caught on a tree root and trips him up.

"Chris watch out!" Selene shouted as she stared in terror as the first guy swung his sword at his head. Barely dodging the sword Chris now had a light cut on his cheek. He looked at his attackers as if he was staring death in his eyes. He slowly got up with his sword pointing at the men as they both round their prey. In a swift movement Chris tripped them up and as they were getting up he knocked one of them out with the hilt of his sword. The other remaining guy swung his sword frantically as Chris approached. Approaching the man defending for his life he took a single swing at the sword and it fell out of the man's hand.

Before further action can be taken he hears a voice. "Yoohoo." The lady called from behind him. Somehow he had forgotten about her as he fought the two men. "You're forgetting about us girls." The lady pouted out before grinning and pulling Selene closer to her body with the dagger against her neck.

"Let her go." He glared as he spoke carefully.

"I'll think about it. So how about we sit down and wait for my friends to wake up." She smiled as she gestures her head towards the conscious men on the ground.

Selene gulped in fear any movement would end her life. The to bulky looking men soon start to wake up after 5 minutes of wait.

"Took you guys long enough." The lady spoke as she walked to them with Selene still trapped in her arms. "Get the prince, we can use him to get more rewards for ourselves."

I have to do something. Selene thought to herself. I don't want to be a burden to the prince. For once, I want to fight. Maybe if I stay beside the prince, I'll find a reason to fight for my life. For once I'll be able to find my purpose of being born into this world, into such a petty life.

Finally finally going through her thoughts she remembered one of the knights in the palace teaching the lady he fancied how to defend herself. Head butt, elbow, stumble, grab, pull, and tuck. She repeated the steps in her head. One...Two...Three... One the last count she did as she thought through.

She swung her head back hitting the Lady straight in the nose before she swung her elbow at her ribcage. The ladies grip started to loosen but Selene head it tight around her shoulders and stumped her toe.

The lady lets out a moan in pain and growls, "Urgh! Bitch!" She swore. Before she could react. Selene held tightly on her arm as she slid one of her legs beneath the lady tucking her upper body into her tummy as if kneeling before a king. In the swift motion the Lady flew forward being flipped and slammed her back to the ground. Her head had hit the ground so hard it bled to the nape of her neck as she grew and stored in rage as her vision hazed.

Selene didn't waste any time, even if she was bleeding in the shoulder and in pain she ran to the prince. The two other guys still didn't know what was happening behind them that they didn't see this coming. Selene had grabbed a log nearby and knocked both the guys on the head. The prince was surprised when he saw Selene, the one he set out to protect saving his ass. She was huffing and puffing and out of breath when she spoke faintly. "We have to go." She grabbed his hand and ran toward the direction she one saw him and Lucy run towards.

Finally out of the forest taking Lucy with them on the way the caught a ride with a merchant and at the gate they were taken to safety. In his arms he held Selene all the way to the castle refusing to let go of the girl who saved his ass.

Back in the forest pissed as hell the lady painted in rage, hate, and anger. "Wait for me Selene...my darling sister."

- To Be Continue -

www.ingramcontent.com/pod-product-compliance
Lightning Source LLC
Chambersburg PA
CBHW020523160726
47991CB00007B/3089